This book belongs to:

....

For Sondra Simon F.S.

For Cicely Culmer J.L.

First published in Great Britain in 2003
by Orion Children's Books
a division of the Orion Publishing Group Ltd
Orion House
5 Upper St Martin's Lane
London WC2H 9EA

Concept, design and illustrations © James Lucas 2003
Text © Francesca Simon 2003

Printed in Italy

LITTLE YELLOW DOG
SAYS LOOK AT ME

WORDS BY FRANCESCA SIMON · PICTURES BY JAMES LUCAS

Orion
Children's Books

Little Yellow Dog strutted down his street.

He chased a leaf.

He swooped on a stick.

He
sniffed
his
favourite
tree.

Then Little Yellow Dog saw something.
Something he had never seen before.

'What's this?'

said Little Yellow Dog.

'Beats me,'
said Ginger Cat.

Little Yellow Dog went a little closer and sniffed.

'It's a bone!
It's a giant bone!'

'Yummy yummy in my tummy!'

said Little Yellow Dog.

He grabbed the bone and tried to pick it up.

'Phooey. It's not a bone,'

said Little Yellow Dog, and pushed it away.

The thing moved.

'Ahhh! It's alive,'

shrieked Little Yellow Dog.

Little Yellow Dog crept closer.

'Come on, chase me!'

The thing didn't answer.

'**OK then, I'll chase you,**' said Little Yellow Dog, pouncing.

'**Whoops!**' said Little Yellow Dog, as the skateboard started to move.

'It's running away with me!'

AIIEEEe!'

He wibbled

and he wobbled

until suddenly. . .

he could do it!

'WHEEEE!

Look at me, Ginger Cat!

I'm flying!"

shouted Little Yellow Dog.

'That was great,'

said Little Yellow Dog, stepping off the skateboard.

WHACK!

SPLAT!

Little Yellow Dog landed
flat on his face.

'Are you **OK?**' said Ginger Cat.

'Fine!' said Little Yellow Dog.

'Look at me!'

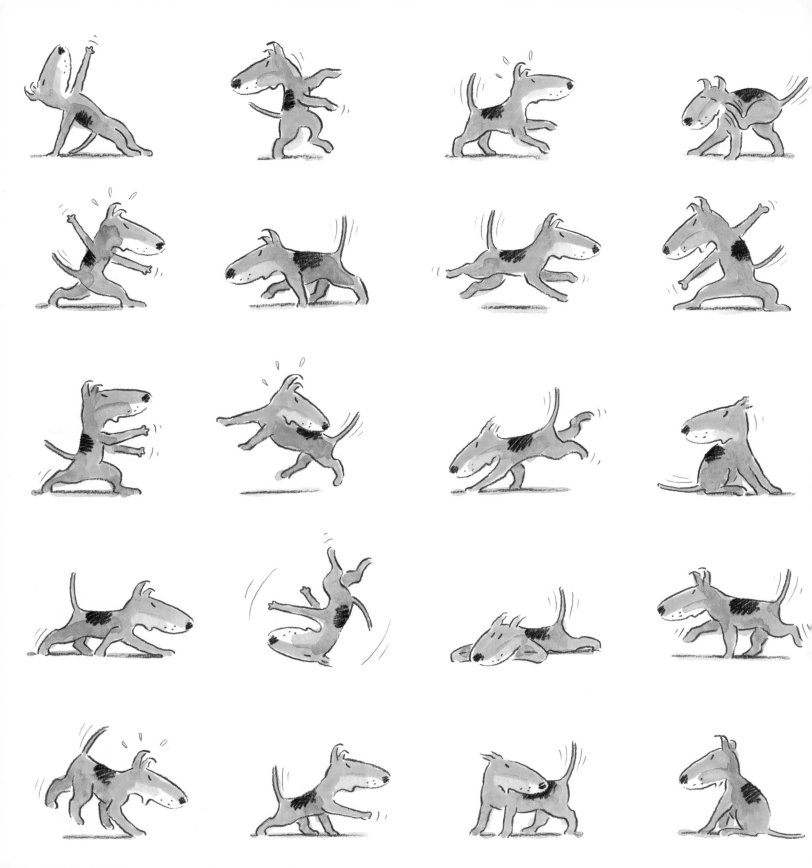